Uprising in Packingtown

Mrigendra Bharti

Published by Sellbrochure Vymish Entertainment, 2024.

UPRISING IN PACKINGTOWN

First edition. July 5, 2024.

Copyright © 2024 Mrigendra Bharti.

ISBN: 979-8227970091

Written by Mrigendra Bharti.

Table of Contents

Preface:

The stench of blood and offal hangs heavy in the air, a constant reminder of the brutal reality of Packingtown. Here, in this labyrinth of slaughterhouses and canneries, dreams are ground to a pulp alongside bone and sinew. Immigrants, lured by the promise of work, find themselves trapped in a relentless cycle of backbreaking labor and meager wages.

But beneath the surface of despair, a flicker of hope ignites. Whispers of rebellion begin to echo through the grimy tenements, carried on the breaths of men and women yearning for a better life. This is the story of those whispers, of how they coalesced into a roar, a testament to the indomitable human spirit in the face of overwhelming odds.

"Uprising in Packingtown" is not merely a historical chronicle; it's a testament to the power of collective action. It delves into the lives of ordinary people – Jurgis, the Lithuanian laborer, Ona, his fiercely determined wife, Mikail, the charismatic organizer, and countless others – as they rise up against the oppressive forces that control their lives.

This is a story of solidarity forged in hardship, of courage blooming in the most unlikely places. It's a reminder that even in the darkest corners, the yearning for justice can spark a revolution. As you turn the pages, prepare to be transported to the heart of Packingtown, a world where the fight for dignity and a better future hangs in the balance.

Prologue:

The acrid tang of blood and decay clung to the air, a thick, fetid fog that permeated every corner of the cavernous space. A symphony of industrial clamor filled the air – the rhythmic thwack of cleavers, the relentless groan of machinery, the guttural bellows of unseen beasts. Under the harsh glare of flickering gaslights, a river of crimson snaked its way across the grease-slick floor, a grim testament to the relentless industry that devoured life whole.

Jurgis trudged through the carnage, his boots squelching against the slick surface. Fatigue gnawed at his bones, a constant companion in this realm of endless toil. Each step was an act of defiance against the relentless rhythm of the slaughterhouse, a silent protest against the dehumanizing nature of his existence.

He glanced around, his eyes scanning the weary faces of his fellow workers. Men of various ethnicities, bound together by the shared experience of hardship and despair. Their expressions were a canvas of exhaustion, resignation, and a flicker of something else – a spark of defiance, a hint of rebellion simmering just beneath the surface.

A haunting melody drifted through the din, a mournful tune hummed by an unseen laborer. The song, a lament for the fallen beasts and a reflection of their own plight, resonated with Jurgis. It was a song of loss, of dreams deferred, and a yearning for a life beyond this blood-soaked purgatory.

As the melody faded, a single word echoed through the cavernous space, whispered from one worker to another, a seed of dissent taking root in the fertile ground of discontent. The word, laden with defiance, held the promise of change – "Union." In the heart of Packingtown, where hope seemed a luxury they could ill afford, a whisper of rebellion had taken root. This whisper, carried on the breath of the downtrodden, would become a roar, a challenge to the brutal machinery that devoured lives and dreams whole. This is the story of that roar, a testament to the unwavering human spirit in the face of overwhelming odds.

About Sellbrochure Vymish Entertainment

Sellbrochure Vymish Entertainment, recognized as India's largest book publishing company, has made significant strides in ensuring its extensive collection of books reaches audiences across the global market. This rapid expansion is a testament to the company's dedication to disseminating knowledge and literature far beyond national borders. Central to its success is its affiliation with InkWhirl Media Networks, a reputable entity in the media and publication industry known for its innovative and strategic approaches. Within this network, InkWhirl Publication LLC operates as a vital division, further enhancing the company's capabilities and reach in the international market.

The visionary behind this enterprise is Mrigendra Bharti, the founder of Sellbrochure Vymish Entertainment. His foresight and passion for the literary world have been instrumental in steering the company towards remarkable growth and recognition. Under his leadership, Sellbrochure Vymish Entertainment has not only expanded its catalog but also established a strong presence in both domestic and international markets. Mrigendra Bharti's commitment to excellence and innovation has been a driving force in the company's journey, ensuring that it stays ahead of industry trends and meets the evolving needs of readers worldwide.

Sellbrochure Vymish Entertainment operates under the robust support of its parental organization, Mrigendra Bharti Group InfoTech. This affiliation provides the necessary resources and strategic guidance, enabling the publishing company to undertake ambitious projects and explore new markets. Mrigendra Bharti Group InfoTech's extensive experience in technology and information services has been a valuable asset, allowing Sellbrochure Vymish Entertainment to integrate advanced digital solutions in its operations, thereby enhancing its distribution capabilities and reader engagement.

Through relentless efforts and a commitment to quality, Sellbrochure Vymish Entertainment continues to break barriers and expand the reach of Indian literature globally. The company's diverse portfolio includes a wide range of genres, catering to different age groups and interests, thereby fostering a rich and inclusive reading culture. As it continues to innovate and grow, Sellbrochure Vymish Entertainment remains dedicated to its mission of making literature accessible to all, contributing significantly to the global literary landscape.

Connect With Mrigendra,
Thank you very much for choosing this book.
You can also connect with me on Instagram,
https://www.instagram.com/i_mrigendrabharti.official
With Love,
Mrigendra Bharti

Introduction:

Packingtown, Illinois. 19—. The very name evokes a cacophony of sounds – the rhythmic thud of cleavers, the ceaseless gurgle of blood, the guttural bellows of unseen beasts. Here, in this labyrinth of slaughterhouses and canneries, the American Dream curdles into a bitter reality for thousands of immigrants. Lured by the promise of work, they find themselves trapped in a relentless cycle of backbreaking labor, meager wages, and a suffocating sense of powerlessness.

This is the story of Jurgis Rudkus, a Lithuanian laborer, and his family, caught in the iron grip of Packingtown. It's a story of dreams deferred, bodies pushed to their limits, and the gnawing sense of injustice that festers beneath the surface of despair.

But amidst the grime and the ceaseless toil, a flicker of hope ignites. Whispers of rebellion begin to echo through the grimy tenements, carried on the breaths of men and women yearning for a better life. This is the story of those whispers, of how they coalesce into a roar, a testament to the indomitable human spirit in the face of overwhelming odds.

"Uprising in Packingtown" isn't just a historical chronicle; it's a visceral journey into the lives of ordinary people. We'll meet Ona, Jurgis' fiercely determined wife, whose unwavering spirit fuels his own resolve. We'll encounter Mikail, the charismatic organizer, whose fiery speeches ignite a spark of hope in the hearts of the downtrodden.

Through their struggles and triumphs, we'll witness the birth of a movement – a testament to the power of collective action. We'll delve into the brutal realities of Packingtown, a world where safety is a luxury and dignity a distant dream. But most importantly, we'll celebrate the enduring human spirit, the yearning for justice that can spark a revolution even in the darkest corners.

Prepare to be transported to the heart of Packingtown, a world where the fight for a better future hangs in the balance. Here, amidst the blood and the offal, where dreams are ground to a pulp alongside bone and sinew, a chorus of voices will rise, demanding change. Turn the page, and let the uprising begin.

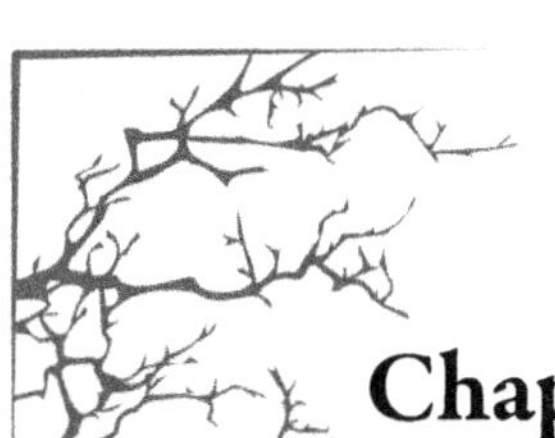

Chapter 1: The Pact

The humid summer air hung heavy over the small town of Ashbrook, a blanket of stillness enveloping the quaint houses and winding streets. As the sun dipped below the horizon, casting long shadows across the landscape, four friends gathered beneath the sprawling canopy of an ancient oak tree, their faces illuminated by the flickering orange glow of a campfire.

Arjun, the self-proclaimed leader of the group, sat with his back against the rough bark, a worn copy of "Treasure Island" clutched in his hand. He was lean and wiry, with eyes that sparkled with an adventurous spirit that seemed to outshine the fire itself. His fingers traced the worn cover of the book, his mind already lost in a world of pirates, buried treasure, and uncharted islands.

Across from him sat Veer, the strategist. Unlike Arjun's impulsive nature, Veer possessed a calm and collected demeanor. His dark brown eyes seemed to miss nothing, constantly scanning their surroundings with a calculating glint. He traced patterns in the dirt with a stick, his mind already formulating plans for their next escapade. His movements were deliberate, each action carefully considered, a testament to his methodical approach.

Next to Veer was Rahul, the joker. A constant stream of jokes and witty remarks flowed from his lips, his laughter echoing through the quiet night. His round face was perpetually creased in a mischievous grin, his eyes twinkling with amusement. He was the glue that held their group together, his lightheartedness a welcome counterpoint to Arjun's seriousness and Veer's stoicism. His presence was infectious, his laughter a balm to their spirits.

Completing the circle was Rohan, the gentle giant. With his broad shoulders and towering height, he exuded an aura of quiet strength. Unlike the others, whose dreams were focused on exploration and adventure, Rohan aspired to become a doctor, his heart filled with a desire to heal and mend. His gentle touch and compassionate nature had earned him the nickname "the healer" among his friends. His presence radiated warmth and kindness, a soothing balm to any troubled soul.

As the embers of the fire crackled and danced, casting dancing shadows on their faces, a comfortable silence settled over them. Arjun, finally tearing his gaze away from the captivating tale of pirates and buried treasure, looked at his friends with a nostalgic smile.

"Remember that time we built a fort in Mrs. Henderson's backyard?" he asked, his voice tinged with a hint of amusement.

A collective chuckle erupted from the group. They vividly recalled the elaborate treehouse they had constructed, complete with a lookout tower and a secret trapdoor. It had been their sanctuary, a place where they could escape the mundane realities of their childhood and embark on imaginary voyages across uncharted seas.

"And how Mrs. Henderson almost caught us climbing the fence?" Rahul chimed in, his voice laced with mock horror. "I swear her stare could curdle milk."

Veer rolled his eyes, a faint smile playing on his lips. "That's why I was the lookout. Never underestimate the power of strategic planning, my friends."

Their laughter mingled with the chirping crickets, a symphony of carefree joy. As the flames subsided, casting an ethereal glow on their faces, Arjun spoke again, his voice turning serious.

"Remember the promise we made that day?" he asked, his gaze fixed on the star-studded sky above.

A hush fell over the group. The playful banter ceased, replaced by a shared memory etched deep in their hearts. The memory of a solemn pact, a vow whispered beneath the rustling leaves of their makeshift fort.

On that warm summer day, perched high above the ground in their makeshift fort, the four friends had made a pact. As they gazed out at the vast expanse of the world before them, their imaginations ignited with possibilities, they swore to embark on an adventure together, an expedition that would take them beyond the boundaries of their small town, into the heart of the unknown.

Arjun, his eyes sparkling with excitement, had declared that they would explore the world's hidden wonders, seeking out lost civilizations and uncovering ancient secrets. Veer, ever the strategist, had envisioned a carefully planned journey, meticulously plotted to maximize their chances of success. Rahul, the joker, had injected his characteristic lightheartedness, promising to bring laughter and joy to their adventure, even amidst the challenges they would face. And Rohan, the gentle giant, had expressed his hope that their journey would not only be one of adventure but also one of service, using their skills and talents to help those in need along the way.

Their pact had been sealed with a handshake, a silent agreement that bound them together, their friendship the foundation upon which their dreams would be built.

Years passed, and the lives of the four friends diverged as they pursued their individual dreams. Arjun, fueled by his insatiable thirst for adventure, climbed mountains, traversed treacherous deserts, and delved into forgotten ruins. He documented his experiences in captivating travelogues, each story igniting a spark of wanderlust in the hearts of his readers.

Veer, with his meticulous mind and strategic thinking, excelled in the world of business. He rose through the ranks of a prestigious corporation, his calculated decisions and keen foresight propelling him to a position of power.

But even amidst the boardrooms and financial reports, a part of him yearned for the thrill of their childhood pact, the promise of an adventure that lay dormant in the back of his mind.

Rahul, ever the charmer, pursued a career in entertainment. His infectious humor and quick wit landed him starring roles in comedies and talk shows. He brought laughter to millions, his face plastered across billboards and magazine covers. Yet, beneath the bright lights and roaring applause, a flicker of longing remained for the simpler times spent with his friends, the anticipation of their shared adventure a secret melody playing in his heart.

Rohan, driven by his unwavering compassion, dedicated himself to medicine. He enrolled in a prestigious medical school, his days filled with grueling studies and late-night shifts at the hospital. His nights were spent tending to the sick and injured, his gentle touch and unwavering dedication bringing comfort and hope to his patients. Despite the demands of his chosen path, the memory of their pact remained a beacon of light, a reminder of the journey they would one day undertake together.

Despite their divergent paths, the bond between the four friends remained strong. They kept in touch regularly, their phone calls and emails filled with updates on their lives and dreams. But a silent yearning lingered beneath the surface, a shared awareness of the unfulfilled promise that hung between them.

One evening, as Arjun sat on the balcony of his hotel room overlooking a bustling Asian city, he received a call from Veer. The usual stoicism in Veer's voice was replaced by a hint of excitement.

"Arjun," Veer began, his voice brimming with newfound energy, "I've been thinking about our pact lately. Remember that jungle adventure we promised ourselves?"

A surge of adrenaline shot through Arjun. He hadn't thought about their childhood vow in years, but the memory of it still held a powerful allure. "Of course, I remember," he replied, his voice echoing Veer's enthusiasm. "Have you been thinking about it too?"

"Absolutely," Veer continued. "With all of us settled in our careers now, maybe it's finally time to make good on our promise. What do you say?"

Arjun's heart pounded with excitement. The years might have passed, but the dream of a shared adventure still burned brightly within him.

"I'm in," he declared without hesitation. "Let's do this."

The call ended, leaving a trail of anticipation in its wake. Arjun knew that convincing Rahul and Rohan wouldn't be easy. Their lives were vastly different from his own, filled with responsibilities and commitments. But he also knew the unyielding strength of their friendship, the bond forged in the fires of childhood dreams.

Fueled by a renewed sense of purpose, Arjun reached out to Rahul and Rohan. Over the next few weeks, they exchanged countless calls and emails, meticulously planning their long-awaited adventure. They debated destinations, meticulously researched potential challenges, and most importantly, rekindled the spirit of camaraderie that had always defined their friendship.

Finally, after months of preparation, a decision was made. Their target: a legendary, uncharted jungle nestled deep in the heart of a remote South American country. The whispers surrounding the jungle were both alluring and unsettling. Tales of breathtaking beauty, hidden ruins, and undiscovered flora and fauna danced alongside rumors of treacherous terrain, hostile wildlife, and ancient curses.

Undeterred by the potential dangers, the four friends made a final pact. They would embark on this adventure together, facing whatever challenges arose with courage, determination, and the unwavering strength of their friendship.

Their childhood promise, a seed planted years ago, was finally ready to blossom into a reality filled with adventure, danger, and the unbreakable bond that tied them together.

THE YEARS LEADING UP to their reunion had been an impressive display of individual triumphs for each friend. Arjun, driven by his insatiable curiosity and adventurous spirit, had become a renowned travel writer. His articles, filled with vivid descriptions and captivating narratives, transported readers to remote corners of the globe. He had climbed Mount Everest, braved the Amazon rainforest, and explored the ancient ruins of Angkor Wat. Each adventure etched a new line on the map of his life, a testament to his unwavering pursuit of experience.

Veer, with his meticulous planning and sharp business acumen, had risen through the ranks of a global corporation, becoming a titan of the financial world. He had mastered the art of strategizing, anticipating market trends, and navigating complex deals. Every decision he made, every risk he calculated, was a calculated step towards an ambitious vision. But amidst the skyscrapers and boardroom meetings, a sliver of his soul remained tethered to the childhood vow, a whisper of adventure that refused to be silenced.

Rahul, with his infectious humor and natural charisma, had become a household name. He had conquered the world of entertainment, starring in hit comedies and hosting highly-rated talk shows. His wit and charm brought laughter to millions, his face adorning billboards and magazine covers. Yet, behind the bright lights and roaring applause, a faint yearning lingered for the simpler times, the days spent plotting their grand adventure with his childhood companions. The memories of their pact remained a source of comfort, a reminder that the true fulfillment lay not in fame but in the bonds of friendship.

Rohan, driven by his unwavering compassion and dedication to healing, had become a respected doctor. He had graduated from one of the most prestigious medical schools in the country, his days filled with grueling studies and late-night shifts at the hospital. His nights were spent tending to the sick and injured, his gentle touch and unwavering dedication bringing comfort and hope to his patients. Despite the demands of his chosen path, the memory of their pact remained a beacon of light, a reminder of the journey they would one day undertake together.

Though their lives had become vastly different, the thread of friendship remained strong. They kept in touch regularly, their phone calls and emails filled with updates on their individual accomplishments and the challenges they faced.

Birthday celebrations were virtual gatherings, filled with laughter and reminiscing about their childhood adventures. Holidays were phone calls, with each friend recounting their experiences, a silent yearning for the time they could share their stories in person.

One evening, as Arjun sat on the terrace of his cozy Airbnb in a bustling Tibetan village, a notification popped up on his phone. It was an email, the subject line simply reading: "The Time Has Come." With a racing heart, he clicked it open. The email was from Veer, written with a passion and excitement Arjun hadn't seen in his friend in years.

"Arjun," the email began, "I've been reminiscing lately. Remember that wild jungle adventure we dreamt about as kids?"

A wave of nostalgia washed over Arjun. He hadn't actively thought about their pact in years, but the memory remained a warm ember in his heart. He tapped out a quick reply, "How could I forget? Have you got something in mind?"

Veer's response came moments later, brimming with excitement. "Not just an idea, Arjun," he wrote, "a plan. I think it's finally time to make good on our promise. What do you say?"

Arjun reread the email several times, a smile slowly spreading across his face. He knew convincing Rahul and Rohan wouldn't be easy. Their lives were far removed from the adventurous spirit of their youth, filled with responsibilities and commitments. But he also knew the unyielding strength of their bond, the pact forged in the fires of childhood dreams. A wave of determination washed over him. He wouldn't let this opportunity slip away.

Driven by a renewed sense of purpose, Arjun reached out to Rahul and Rohan. Over the next few weeks, their communication increased – a flurry of phone calls, video chats, and emails. They meticulously planned their long-awaited adventure, discussing destinations, researching potential hazards, and most importantly, rekindling the spirit of camaraderie that had always defined their friendship.

Their initial conversations were filled with practicality and logistical challenges. Rahul was hesitant, worried about taking a break from his demanding schedule and the potential financial strain. Rohan, ever the cautious one, expressed concerns about the risks of venturing into an uncharted jungle. Yet, as they talked, the fire of excitement began to flicker within them too.

Arjun, his voice brimming with enthusiasm, painted vivid pictures of hidden wonders and unexplored territories. Veer, ever the planner, outlined their meticulously researched itinerary, ensuring they were prepared for any potential obstacles.

Finally, after months of discussions and countless revisions, a decision was made. Their target: the mythical El Dorado,

Their target wasn't just any adventure; it was the legendary lost city of El Dorado, rumored to be nestled deep within the heart of a remote South American jungle. The whispers surrounding El Dorado were both alluring and unsettling. Tales of breathtaking beauty, hidden temples overflowing with gold, and undiscovered flora and fauna danced alongside rumors of treacherous terrain, hostile wildlife, and ancient curses guarding the city's secrets.

Undeterred by the potential dangers, the four friends made a final pact over a video call, their faces etched with a mixture of excitement and apprehension. They would embark on this adventure together, facing whatever challenges arose with courage, determination, and the unwavering strength of their friendship. Their childhood promise, a seed planted years ago, was finally ready to blossom into a reality filled with adventure, danger, and the unbreakable bond that tied them together.

Months of meticulous planning followed. Drawing on their individual strengths, they divided the tasks. Arjun, the seasoned explorer, handled the research, meticulously studying maps, gathering information about the region, and identifying potential routes into the jungle. Veer, the strategist, secured permits, hired local guides, and acquired the necessary equipment, ensuring they had everything they needed to survive in the harsh jungle environment.

Rahul, ever the optimist, handled morale and logistics. He compiled a first-aid kit, packed emergency supplies, and created a communication plan, a lifeline to the outside world in case of unforeseen emergencies. Rohan, the pragmatist, secured medical supplies and focused on their physical conditioning, ensuring they were prepared for the grueling physical demands of the trek.

As the departure date approached, a sense of frenetic energy filled their lives. Arjun, usually meticulous in his packing, found himself throwing essentials into a backpack with haphazard haste. Veer, his usual calm demeanor slightly ruffled, double-checked every detail of their itinerary, ensuring nothing was left to chance. Rahul, despite his outward excitement, masked a flicker of nervous energy with an onslaught of jokes and witty remarks. Rohan, ever the voice of reason, kept them grounded, reminding them of the potential dangers and the importance of staying focused.

Finally, the day arrived. With a flurry of goodbyes and promises to stay in touch, they boarded their separate flights, their hearts pounding with a mix of anticipation and apprehension. They were finally on their way to fulfill their childhood pact, a journey that would test their friendship, their courage, and their very survival.

As their planes touched down in the bustling South American capital, they were greeted by a wall of humid air and a cacophony of unfamiliar sights and sounds. Reunions were filled with excitement and nervous laughter, their individual anxieties dissolving in the warmth of their shared purpose.

Their first task was to meet with their guide, a weathered local named Miguel, who possessed an intimate knowledge of the treacherous jungle. Miguel, a man of few words, surveyed them with a critical eye, assessing their fitness and preparedness. After a grueling negotiation (conducted mostly by Veer), Miguel agreed to lead them into the heart of the jungle.

The next few days were a blur of activity. They purchased last-minute supplies, hired a team of porters to carry their heavy backpacks, and acclimatized themselves to the city's sweltering heat. Finally, the day of departure arrived.

Packed into a beat-up jeep, they rattled down dusty roads, leaving the comfort of civilization behind. As the city faded into the distance, swallowed by the encroaching jungle, the reality of their adventure settled in. They were about to embark on a journey unlike any they had ever experienced, a journey that would redefine their friendship and test the limits of their courage.

Chapter 2: Into the Unknown

The jeep sputtered to a halt, its engine coughing one last time before falling silent. Dust swirled around them, momentarily obscuring the dense wall of vegetation that marked the entrance to the jungle. Stepping out of the vehicle, the four friends were greeted by a cacophony of unfamiliar sounds: the raucous squawks of unseen birds, the incessant drone of insects, and the low, guttural growls that seemed to emanate from the depths of the undergrowth. The air hung heavy with humidity, thick enough to taste, and the sunlight struggled to pierce the dense canopy overhead, casting the forest floor in a perpetual twilight.

A bead of sweat trickled down Arjun's temple. He adjusted his backpack, the weight of their supplies a constant reminder of the arduous journey ahead. Despite the initial apprehension, a spark of excitement danced in his eyes. This was the world he craved, a place where adventure lurked around every bend and the unknown waited to be unveiled.

Veer, ever the pragmatist, scanned their surroundings with a practiced eye. He surveyed the towering trees, their gnarled branches reaching towards the sky like skeletal fingers, and the tangled undergrowth that seemed determined to impede their progress. A frown etched itself onto his face. This was not an ordinary forest; it was a living, breathing entity, a maze of emerald green that promised both beauty and danger.

Rahul, usually the life of the party, was uncharacteristically quiet. He nervously chewed on his lip, his gaze darting from the towering trees to the unseen creatures stirring in the undergrowth. Jokes usually flowed from him like a spring, but in the face of this overwhelming wilderness, his usual lightheartedness was replaced by a cautious silence.

Rohan, the voice of reason, placed a reassuring hand on Rahul's shoulder. "Don't worry," he said, his voice calm and steady. "We're in this together. Remember, we planned for this." His quiet strength offered a sense of stability amidst the initial trepidation.

Their guide, Miguel, a man whose weathered face mirrored the landscape around them, stood impassive, his gaze fixed on a point unseen. He grunted once, a sound that spoke volumes, and gestured towards a barely discernible path weaving through the dense foliage. This was their entrance, a portal into a world shrouded in mystery.

With a deep breath, Arjun shouldered his backpack and stepped onto the path. The others followed suit, a single file cutting through the thick undergrowth. The air grew cooler as the sunlight struggled to penetrate the dense canopy. The jungle floor was a damp, earthy carpet, littered with decaying leaves and the occasional fallen log. Strange, iridescent insects buzzed around their heads, their buzzing adding to the symphony of sounds that filled the air.

As they ventured deeper, the path became even more treacherous. Twisted vines snagged at their clothes, and thorny bushes scratched at their exposed skin. The air grew thick with the cloying scent of decaying vegetation, a smell that clung to their clothes and filled their nostrils. The silence, broken only by the rustle of leaves beneath their feet and the occasional bird call, began to feel oppressive, a weight pressing down on them.

Hours melted into a blur of green. Time seemed to lose its meaning amidst the dense foliage. The monotony of the scenery and the relentless dampness began to wear on their spirits. Yet, they pressed on, driven by a shared determination and the unyielding promise that lay at the heart of the jungle.

Suddenly, the dense foliage thinned out, and they found themselves standing on the bank of a wide, slow-moving river. The water was a deep brown, reflecting the dark canopy above like a polished mirror. Fallen logs and branches formed a precarious bridge across the span, a rickety crossing that looked more like an obstacle course than a safe passage.

Miguel, their guide, assessed the bridge with a practiced eye. He pointed at several protruding branches and mumbled something in Spanish. Arjun, who had learned a smattering of the language during his travels, translated. "He says these are the strongest points to hold onto."

Fear momentarily clouded Rahul's judgment. "There has to be another way, right?" he said, his voice strained. "This looks...unsafe."

Veer, ever the strategist, stepped forward. "There isn't," he said flatly. "This is the only way across." He eyed the bridge, a plan already forming in his mind.

Rohan, ever the pragmatist, knelt by the riverbank and studied the water. "We need to be careful," he said "...There could be currents or hidden dangers below the surface. Miguel, can you tell if the water is deep?"

Miguel grunted noncommittally and tossed a small pebble into the river. They watched as it skipped across the surface for a few seconds before disappearing with a tiny plop. The lack of a splash was unsettling.

"Alright," Veer announced, taking charge. "We'll cross one at a time. Arjun, you go first. Use those strong branches Miguel pointed out, and take your time."

Arjun took a deep breath, his stomach churning with a mix of excitement and apprehension. He gripped the rough bark of the first protruding branch, the damp wood slick in his sweating palms. Stepping onto the bridge, he cautiously shifted his weight, testing its stability. The bridge creaked and groaned under his weight, sending shivers down his spine. He inched forward, clinging to the branches with all his might. Each step was a gamble, a dance with potential disaster.

The others watched with bated breath as Arjun crossed the treacherous bridge. Rahul, unable to bear the suspense, paced back and forth along the riverbank, muttering encouragement under his breath. Rohan kept his gaze fixed on Arjun, ready to react if he lost his footing.

After what seemed like an eternity, Arjun finally reached the other side. Relief washed over him as he stood on solid ground, his legs trembling slightly from the exertion. He grinned back at his friends, offering them a thumbs-up sign.

One by one, they followed suit. Veer crossed with his usual calm efficiency, his movements calculated and precise. Rahul, a ball of nervous energy, fumbled his way across, muttering jokes under his breath to mask his fear. Rohan, ever the cautious one, took his time, carefully placing each foot on the sturdiest points.

Finally, they were all safely reunited on the opposite bank. They stood for a moment, catching their breath and letting the adrenaline subside. The ordeal had been a baptism by fire, a stark reminder of the challenges that lay ahead.

As they continued their trek, the landscape began to change subtly. The dense undergrowth thinned out, replaced by a network of towering trees with smooth, barkless trunks. Sunlight pierced through the canopy in sporadic shafts, illuminating patches of the forest floor with an ethereal glow. The air grew warmer and drier, carrying with it a strange sweetness that tickled their senses.

Suddenly, Miguel stopped in his tracks. He pointed towards a cluster of trees unlike any they had seen before. Their bark was a vibrant crimson, and large, trumpet-shaped flowers bloomed in shades of purple and orange. The air around them hummed with the buzzing of unseen insects, attracted to the sweet nectar.

Arjun's eyes widened with excitement. "What are those?" he whispered, his voice filled with awe.

Miguel shook his head, unable to answer. He clearly had never encountered these plants before. Arjun whipped out his camera, capturing the scene in digital memory. He knew that documenting this unique ecosystem would be a valuable contribution to the world of botany.

As they ventured deeper into this new section of the jungle, they stumbled upon even more wonders. They encountered a clearing where a family of brightly colored parrots squawked playfully in the branches. They followed a winding path that led them past a crystal-clear stream cascading down moss-covered rocks.

Each new discovery fueled their sense of wonder, each step revealing a hidden treasure of the jungle's rich biodiversity.

However, the beauty of the jungle was not without its perils. As dusk began to settle, casting long shadows across the forest floor, they heard a series of unsettling growls emanating from the dense undergrowth. The sounds were guttural, low-pitched, and undeniably menacing.

A shiver ran down Rahul's spine. "What was that?" he whispered, his voice barely audible.

Veer, ever vigilant, scanned the surrounding trees, his eyes searching for the source of the sound. Rohan reached into his backpack and pulled out a headlamp, its beam cutting through the gathering darkness.

Miguel, his usually stoic expression replaced by a flicker of concern, spoke in rapid Spanish. Arjun, his Spanish rusty but functional, managed to translate. "He says it's a pack of jaguars," he said, his voice betraying a hint of worry.

The revelation sent a jolt of fear through the group. Jaguars were apex predators, solitary hunters known for their stealth and power. An encounter with a pack would be a fight for survival.

As they stood frozen, unsure of their next move, the growls grew louder, closer. The jungle, once a source of wonder, now felt like a menacing labyrinth, filled with unseen dangers. They had ventured too far, entered a territory where they were not welcome.

Suddenly, a guttural shriek pierced the air, unlike anything they'd heard before. It was high-pitched and almost human-sounding, followed by a series of furious screeches. Confused, they exchanged nervous glances. The jaguars seemed distracted, their growls momentarily replaced by a new, unknown threat.

Miguel, ever the seasoned guide, pointed towards the source of the commotion. Through the dense foliage, they could barely make out a blur of movement - a dark shape darting between the trees. It was too dark to see anything clearly, but the size and agility suggested a large primate, possibly a spider monkey.

Then, another sound emerged from the depths of the jungle - a series of deep, guttural growls entirely different from the jaguars' calls. This new growl was a low rumble that vibrated through their bones, a primal sound that spoke of immense power and a ferocious hunger.

Panic gripped them. They were caught in a three-way stand-off, the jaguars, the unknown primate, and a terrifying third predator they couldn't even identify. The air crackled with tension, the symphony of the jungle replaced by a cacophony of fear.

"We need to get out of here," Veer declared, his voice cutting through the panic. "Now!"

Reacting with a newfound urgency, they followed Miguel as he plunged deeper into the undergrowth. Thorns ripped at their clothes, branches lashed at their faces, but they pushed forward, fueled by the primal urge to survive. The growls of the unseen predator followed them, a constant reminder of the danger they were running from.

After what felt like an eternity, they stumbled into a clearing. Moonlight filtered through the canopy, bathing the area in an ethereal glow. In the center stood a towering ancient tree, its gnarled branches reaching towards the sky like skeletal fingers. Miguel pointed towards a hollow at the base of the tree, a large enough space for them to all squeeze inside.

Without hesitation, they scrambled towards the tree, using roots and vines to hoist themselves up. Once inside the hollow, they huddled together, their chests heaving with exertion and fear. The air inside was stale and musty, but it offered a temporary reprieve from the dangers of the jungle floor.

Crouched in the darkness, they listened intently to the sounds emanating from outside. The growls of the jaguars had faded, replaced by the occasional shriek from the unknown primate. The deep, unsettling growls of the third predator, however, were still audible, closer now, circling the clearing.

A cold dread settled over them. Fear had morphed into a primal terror, the kind that gnawed at your insides and left your limbs trembling. They were trapped, prey in a game they didn't understand, surrounded by unseen dangers.

As they huddled together in the darkness, a question hung heavy in the air: would they survive the night, or would they become another victim of the jungle's unforgiving wilderness?

The Night Unfolds

The night stretched on interminably, each tick of Arjun's wristwatch echoing like a death knell. Hours blurred into one another, filled with the tense anticipation of the unknown predator's return. Sleep was a fleeting dream, replaced by a constant vigil against the unseen threat.

Rahul, usually the joker, was uncharacteristically silent. He sat huddled next to Rohan, his eyes wide with terror. Even the ever-stoic Veer couldn't mask the worry etched on his face. Arjun, despite his bravado, felt a knot of fear twisting in his gut.

Suddenly, a loud screech pierced the silence. They all flinched, adrenaline jolting through their system. The unknown primate, the apparent target of the predator, was much closer now, its shrieks filled with a desperate pleading.

Then, another sound filled the night - a bone-chilling growl, so close it seemed to vibrate through the very ground they were huddled on. The predator had found its prey. A horrifying struggle ensued, a cacophony of shrieks and snarls that sent shivers down their spines. They could almost picture the brutal fight unfolding outside, the predator's raw power against the desperate struggles of the primate.

The fight was short-lived. The shrieks abruptly stopped, replaced by a sickening silence. The predator had triumphed. A heavy silence descended, broken only by the labored breathing of the four friends huddled together in the darkness.

The tension remained thick in the air. They knew the predator could easily turn its attention towards them next. The night, already filled with terror, became even more unbearable.

As the hours dragged on, they began to lose hope. Dawn seemed like an eternity away, and the predator lurked outside, a silent, unseen threat waiting for them to emerge.

Just when despair threatened to consume them, a faint glimmer of light peeked through the dense foliage, announcing the long-awaited arrival of dawn. Relief washed over them like a tidal wave. The night, filled with terror and uncertainty, was finally over.

With newfound energy, they clambered out of the hollow, their legs stiff and their bodies aching. The clearing looked different in the harsh light of day. The beauty of the ancient tree was overshadowed by the chilling reminder of the events that transpired the night before.

Miguel, his face etched with worry, surveyed the scene. He pointed at a trail of blood leading away from the base of the tree, a grim testament to the predator's victory. Relief mingled with a sense of unease. They may have survived the night, but the danger was far from over.

As they discussed their next course of action, a sense of discord settled amongst them. Arjun, the adventurer, yearned to press on, driven by the unfulfilled promise of El Dorado. Veer, the pragmatist, argued for caution, prioritizing their safety over their goal. Rahul, shaken to his core by the previous night's events, expressed his desire to abandon the mission and return to civilization. Rohan, the voice of reason, suggested a compromise: explore for another day, but remain vigilant and prepared to turn back at the first sign of danger.

After a tense debate, they reached a decision. They would continue their journey for one more day, staying close to Miguel for guidance and relying on their heightened sense of awareness. It was a fragile agreement, a balance between their adventurous spirit and the ever-present threat lurking in the jungle.

As they ventured deeper, the landscape began to transform. The dense undergrowth gave way to a network of towering sandstone cliffs, their weathered surfaces etched with mysterious symbols. The air grew cooler, carrying with it a faint scent of minerals and damp earth. The sunlight, diffused through the canopy, cast long shadows across the uneven terrain, lending an air of mystery to the surroundings.

Suddenly, Miguel stopped in his tracks, his hand raised in a silent signal. He pointed towards a narrow crevice between two towering cliffs. A shaft of sunlight illuminated the opening, revealing a narrow passage that seemed to disappear into the heart of the rock formation.

A wave of excitement surged through Arjun.

Could this be a hidden entrance, a pathway leading them closer to El Dorado? Miguel, however, seemed hesitant. He muttered something in Spanish, shaking his head slowly.

Arjun, his curiosity piqued, translated for the others. "He says it's a sacred place for his people," Arjun explained, "a place of spirits and forbidden knowledge."

A flicker of apprehension crossed Rohan's face. "Maybe we should just keep going," he suggested, "there's gotta be another way around these cliffs."

Veer, however, saw the potential value in exploring the crevice. "Perhaps," he said, his voice filled with an undercurrent of excitement, "this could be a shortcut, a way to bypass the treacherous terrain ahead. Miguel, can you assess the safety of entering the crevice?"

Miguel remained unconvinced, but after a heated debate, he reluctantly agreed to scout the passage. He disappeared into the crevice, his figure swallowed by the darkness. The silence that followed was heavy with anticipation.

Moments that felt like an eternity stretched into minutes. Just as their patience began to wear thin, a faint shout echoed from within the crevice. Miguel reappeared, a look of astonishment etched on his face.

"You have to see this," he exclaimed, his voice filled with a mixture of awe and trepidation. "Come, follow me."

Hesitantly, they followed Miguel into the narrow passage. Stooping low, they navigated the darkness, relying on their headlamps to illuminate their path. The air grew cooler, damp, and carried a strange, ancient smell. The passage twisted and turned, a labyrinth carved into the heart of the rock.

After what seemed like an age, they emerged into a hidden chamber. The sight that greeted them was breathtaking. The chamber was carved from smooth, reddish sandstone, its walls adorned with intricate murals depicting scenes of a lost civilization. Strange symbols, similar to those etched on the cliff face outside, were etched into the floor. In the center of the chamber stood a massive obsidian monolith, its surface reflecting the faint glow of their headlamps with an otherworldly sheen.

A hush fell over the group as they stood mesmerized by the sight. This hidden chamber was a testament to a bygone era, a glimpse into a civilization shrouded in mystery. The air crackled with an energy that sent shivers down their spines.

As they marveled at the chamber's beauty, a faint rustling sound broke the silence. It came from the shadows at the far end of the room, unseen and unsettling. Their hearts pounded in their chests, their headlamps frantically searching the darkness.

A tall, slender figure emerged from the shadows, cloaked in a garment woven from vibrant feathers. Its head was obscured by a feathered mask, leaving only penetrating eyes visible. The figure spoke in a language that sounded melodic yet utterly foreign, a language filled with clicks and whistles unlike anything they had ever heard.

Miguel, his face pale with shock, stepped forward. He spoke in rapid Spanish, his voice a mixture of fear and respect. Arjun, bewildered, translated. "He says... it's a guardian of this place," Arjun stammered, "a protector of the secrets."

The figure remained still, its eyes fixed on them. The air crackled with tension as a delicate dance of uncertainty unfolded. Were these guardians hostile or merely protectors?

Suddenly, the figure held out its hand, palm open. In its grasp lay a small, intricately carved stone tablet. The symbols etched on the tablet were similar to those adorning the chamber walls.

Miguel, his voice barely above a whisper, explained. "He offers a choice," he said, "a test. This tablet holds a riddle. If you answer correctly, he will allow you passage. If you fail..." he trailed off, leaving the unspoken threat hanging in the air.

A wave of fear washed over them. Another challenge, another unknown variable in their already perilous journey. Yet, the lure of El Dorado remained strong, and the thought of turning back now was unbearable.

Veer, the ever-strategist, stepped forward. "Let's hear the riddle," he said, his voice surprisingly calm. "We'll work it out together."

The guardian tilted its head, a gesture that could be interpreted as either approval or curiosity. Then, it spoke in its strange language, a series of clicks and whistles that resonated throughout the chamber.

As the last syllable faded, silence descended once more. The four friends huddled together, their faces etched with apprehension. They didn't understand the language, the riddle remained a mystery.

Suddenly, a flicker of recognition crossed Arjun's face. During his research, he had stumbled upon an ancient text that mentioned a lost civilization and their language, a language filled with unusual sounds and tonal variations. He vaguely remembered a fragment of the text, a sentence that resonated with the sequence of clicks and whistles used by the guardian.

Hope flared in his eyes. He relayed his memory to his friends, translating the fragment of the text as best he could. It was a proverb, a saying about the value of knowledge and the importance of respecting the past.

With a collective breath, they turned towards the guardian. Arjun spoke the proverb in his best approximation of the clicking language, hoping it would be enough.

The chamber fell silent. The guardian remained unmoving, its gaze fixed on them. Then, a slow smile seemed to spread across its masked face. It inclined its head once more, a gesture of approval. The tension in the room eased, replaced by a sense of wonder.

The guardian placed the stone tablet in Arjun's hand, a tangible reward for their success. It then turned and walked back into the shadows, disappearing from sight as swiftly as it had appeared.

The chamber doors opened, revealing a hidden passage leading deeper into the rock formation. It was a path less traveled, a secret known only to the guardians and potentially leading closer to El Dorado.

Excitement and apprehension warred within them. They had passed the test, but their journey was far from over. This hidden chamber, with its murals, monolith, and cryptic tablet, presented a new set of challenges. Would the tablet be a key, unlocking the secrets of El Dorado? Or was it a mere obstacle, another test on their path?

One thing was certain - their adventure had taken an unexpected turn. They were no longer just explorers searching for a lost city; they were becoming part of a story far more ancient and mysterious than they ever imagined.

As they stood at the threshold of the hidden passage, a sense of destiny beckoned them forward. They looked at each other, a silent pact forming between them. They would face whatever challenges lay ahead, unravel the secrets of the tablet, and continue their quest for El Dorado.

With newfound determination, they stepped into the passage, leaving behind the chamber and its guardian. The unknown awaited them, a labyrinth of secrets and dangers, leading them deeper into the heart of the ancient jungle.

Chapter 3: The Heart of Packingtown

The stench hit Jurgis before he even saw the stockyards. It was a thick, cloying odor that clung to the air, a nauseating cocktail of blood, manure, and decay. He wrinkled his nose and coughed, regretting the hearty breakfast of sausage and potatoes he'd devoured earlier that morning.

As they approached the gates of Brown's Packing Company, the enormity of the operation slammed into them like a physical blow. Endless lines of cattle snaked towards massive brick buildings, their moos blending into a cacophony of fear and distress. Men, their faces hardened and clothes spattered with blood, barked orders and wielded electric prods, herding the animals with practiced cruelty.

Jurgis gulped, a knot of unease forming in his stomach. The idealistic visions he'd harbored about America, the land of opportunity and abundance, were quickly dissipating. This was a brutal, unforgiving world, far removed from the pastoral scenes he'd imagined.

Ona, clutching Teta Elzbieta's arm, squeezed her hand tightly. Her eyes flickered with fear, a stark contrast to her usual vibrant spirit. Even Dede Antanas, usually stoic and silent, seemed overwhelmed by the sheer scale of the operation.

Jokubas, however, seemed strangely at ease. He greeted a burly man with a thick mustache and a bloodstained apron in a language Jurgis didn't recognize. After a brief conversation, the man nodded towards a building labeled "Employment Office" and ushered them inside.

The office was a cramped, dimly lit space with a line of men snaking out the door. The air hung heavy with the smell of sweat, tobacco, and cheap liquor. Jurgis pushed his way through the throng, his Lithuanian a beacon of familiarity in a sea of unfamiliar languages.

The clerk behind the counter, a man with a greasy comb-over and a bored expression, barely glanced up as he saw them. He barked a question in English, his voice devoid of warmth.

Jokubas, ever the resourceful one, stepped forward and explained their situation, using a mix of Lithuanian and broken English. The clerk listened impatiently, then scribbled something on a piece of paper and thrust it towards Jurgis.

"Shoveler," it read in bold lettering. Jurgis stared at the word, his heart sinking. A shoveler? He, a skilled carpenter, was to be reduced to scooping up blood and entrails? Disappointment gnawed at him, but the promise of steady work, however unpleasant, outweighed his pride.

As they were ushered out of the office, a group of younger men swaggered in, their clothes new and their faces clean-shaven. They spoke in an American dialect Jurgis was unfamiliar with, their voices filled with bravado. One of them, spotting the Lithuanian family, gave them a sneering look.

"Greenhorns," he muttered under his breath, a derogatory term that sent a shiver down Jurgis' spine.

Jokubas, sensing their apprehension, placed a hand on Jurgis' shoulder. "Don't worry, young one," he said, his voice low but firm. "This is just the beginning. We'll find our way here. We always do."

Jurgis nodded, forcing a smile. He knew his father was right. They had faced hardship before, and they had emerged stronger. But this... this was different. This was a world that seemed designed to break a man, to chew him up and spit him out.

Following another burly man with a blood-stained cleaver, they were led through a maze of corridors, the smell of death intensifying with every step. Finally, they reached a vast open space filled with a horrifying spectacle.

Hundreds of cattle carcasses hung from hooks, their flesh stripped bare, their insides spilling out in a grotesque display. Men with calloused hands and steely expressions hacked away at the meat, a bloody ballet of dismemberment. The floor was slick with animal fat and gore, reflecting the harsh overhead lights in a sickening sheen.

Jurgis felt his stomach churn. This wasn't the honest work he had envisioned. This was a scene from a nightmare, a glimpse into the industrial underbelly of the American dream.

The foreman, a man with a thick scar across his cheek and a missing tooth, pointed towards a pile of shovels and assigned them their tasks. Jurgis picked up a shovel, the cold metal biting into his hand. He hefted it, feeling its weight settle against his shoulder. This was his new reality. This was Packingtown.

As Jurgis joined the other men, shoveling entrails into a waiting vat, a single thought echoed in his mind: how long could he endure this?

The air hung heavy with the metallic tang of blood, the incessant buzz of flies, and the chorus of grunts and curses from the men around him. Jurgis shoveled tirelessly, his muscles screaming in protest with each scoop. The entrails were slick and cold, leaving a trail of slime on his clothes and boots. The constant exposure to death, the raw, exposed flesh stripped of its life force, chipped away at his spirit.

He glanced around at his fellow workers. Some, like himself, were new arrivals, their faces a mixture of fear and disgust.

Others were seasoned veterans, their expressions hardened into a mask of indifference. A man with one eye and a limp, whom everyone called "Lefty," took pity on Jurgis' struggle.

"Take your time, greenhorn," he rasped, his voice worn from years of shouting over the din. "The faster you try to go, the worse the mess you'll make.

Jurgis nodded his thanks, wiping sweat from his brow. "How long have you been here, Lefty?" he asked, his voice barely a whisper above the surrounding clamor.

"Long enough, son," Lefty replied with a humorless chuckle. "Long enough to see men come and go, dreams turn to dust." His words were a grim warning, a glimpse of the future that awaited Jurgis if he didn't find a way to cope.

As the hours dragged on, the relentless work took its toll. Jurgis' back ached, his arms burned, and his stomach churned with nausea. He stumbled once, nearly falling into the vat of entrails, the stench nearly knocking him unconscious. A chorus of jeers erupted from the other workers, a cruel reminder of his greenhorn status.

Suddenly, a piercing shriek sliced through the din. Jurgis looked up to see a young man, barely older than himself, struggling in the grip of a burly foreman. The foreman was yelling something, his face contorted in rage.

"He didn't hear the bell," a bystander explained. "New guy, doesn't know the rules."

The bell, Jurgis realized with a jolt, was a faint, almost inaudible clang that signaled a break. He hadn't even noticed it in the haze of exhaustion.

The foreman shoved the young man towards a dangling chain, a contraption used to hoist slaughtered animals. Jurgis watched in horror as the young man was lifted high above the ground, his screams muffled by a rag stuffed in his mouth.

A wave of defiance surged through Jurgis. This cruelty, this blatant disregard for human life, was more than he could stomach. Before he could think twice, he dropped his shovel and charged towards the foreman, adrenaline fueling his steps.

"Leave him alone!" Jurgis roared, his voice raw with anger.

The foreman turned, a surprised look on his scarred face. The other workers stopped working, their gaze fixed on the unfolding scene. Time seemed to slow down.

"Who the hell are you?" the foreman snarled, his voice dripping with menace.

Jurgis stood his ground, his fists clenched. "A man," he declared, his voice trembling slightly. "A man who won't stand by and watch this kind of treatment."

For a moment, it seemed like the foreman would launch himself at Jurgis. Then, a flicker of something akin to respect crossed his face. He shoved the young man aside, the chain clanging as it lowered him to the floor.

"New blood," the foreman muttered, spitting a glob of tobacco juice onto the ground. "Always got somethin' to prove."

He turned away and stalked off, leaving Jurgis standing there, his heart pounding in his chest. The other workers watched him with a mix of curiosity and admiration. Lefty gave him a slow nod, a silent acknowledgement of his bravery.

Jurgis had taken a stand, a small act of defiance against the brutal system of Packingtown. It was a moment of clarity, a realization that even in this oppressive environment, there was still a flicker of humanity left. But he knew this was just the beginning. The true test of his spirit, his endurance, was yet to come. The heart of Packingtown was a place that devoured dreams and crushed hope. He had a long road ahead, and it wouldn't be easy.

As he picked up his shovel and resumed his work, a steely resolve settled in Jurgis' eyes. He would not be broken. He would survive this place, and one day, he would rise above it. He would find a way to build a better life for himself, Ona, and their family. But for now, he had to focus on the present, on surviving another day in the unforgiving heart of Packingtown.

The day wore on, an eternity of blood, sweat, and exhaustion. As the final whistle blew, signaling the end of the shift, Jurgis felt like his body had been put through a meat grinder. His muscles screamed in protest, his hands were blistered and raw, and the stench of death clung to him like a shroud.

Emerging from the slaughterhouse, he was greeted by a sight that surprised him. A small group of Lithuanian immigrants, men and women alike, huddled together under a flickering gas lamp. Jokubas was amongst them, a steaming mug of something warm clasped in his hand.

Relief washed over Jurgis. He hadn't realized how desperately he had craved a connection, a familiar voice in this alien land. He stumbled towards them, his legs shaky and his spirit yearning for a shred of comfort.

"There you are, young one," Jokubas greeted him, a warm smile creasing his weathered face. "We were worried sick."

He handed Jurgis a mug, the steam carrying the inviting aroma of herbal tea. Jurgis took a grateful sip, the warmth soothing his raw throat. He looked at the others, their faces etched with fatigue but their eyes holding a spark of fellowship.

Ona rushed towards him, her eyes filled with concern. She fussed over him, wiping the grime from his face and checking for any injuries. He saw a mixture of worry and pride in her gaze.

"You stood up for the young one," Dede Antanas rasped, his voice gravelly but his eyes holding a flicker of respect. "That took courage."

Jurgis nodded, the memory of the incident still raw in his mind. He felt a pang of guilt for his outburst, unsure if it was a foolhardy act of defiance or a necessary display of humanity.

"We all have to look out for each other here," a woman named Marija spoke up, her voice soft but filled with a quiet strength. "This place will try to break you, but we have to hold onto our humanity, onto our community."

Her words resonated with Jurgis. He looked around at the group, these strangers who were suddenly his lifeline. They were all in the same boat - battered, bruised, but determined to survive. In their shared struggle, he found a glimmer of hope, a sense of belonging he hadn't expected in this brutal world.

As they talked, sharing stories of their journeys, their families back home, and the harsh realities of Packingtown, a sense of solidarity grew. Jokubas produced a worn deck of cards, and soon they were lost in a game of Spitoon, a familiar Lithuanian pastime. Laughter, albeit strained, filled the air, a small rebellion against the oppressive atmosphere.

The meager stew Ona had prepared back at their cramped tenement tasted like a feast. Huddled together for warmth, Jurgis felt a sense of gratitude for his family, for their love and unwavering support. They were his anchor, a reminder of the life he was fighting for.

As he drifted off to sleep, exhausted but strangely hopeful, Jurgis knew that Packingtown would be a long, arduous journey. But he also knew he wasn't alone. He had his family, his newfound community, and a newfound spark of defiance burning within him. He would face the challenges of the coming days, one grueling shift at a time, with the hope of a brighter future guiding his way. The heart of Packingtown might be a place of darkness, but within it, flickered the embers of resilience, of human connection, that would keep him going.

Days bled into weeks, each one a monotonous cycle of backbreaking labor, foul smells, and aching muscles. Jurgis had become accustomed to the rhythm of Packingtown, his body a finely tuned machine for shoveling entrails. Yet, the harshness of the work never dulled, the brutality never truly faded.

One evening, after another grueling shift, Jurgis found himself drawn to a hushed conversation taking place in a dimly lit corner of the boarding house. A group of men, mostly Slavic immigrants, were huddled around a flickering candle, whispering amongst themselves. Curiosity tugged at Jurgis, and he hesitantly approached the group.

"Mind if I join you?" he asked, his voice barely a whisper.

A man with a neatly trimmed mustache and piercing blue eyes looked up. "Come, sit," he beckoned, gesturing to a crate. "New here, I see."

Jurgis nodded, introducing himself and explaining that he was Lithuanian. The man introduced himself as Mikail, a Polish immigrant who had been working at Packingtown for several years.

The group, Jurgis soon learned, was discussing a growing movement amongst the workers - whispers of a union. The idea of organized resistance against the harsh working conditions and low wages sparked a flicker of hope within Jurgis. Was this the answer they'd been searching for? A way to fight back against the oppressive system that chewed them up and spat them out?

Mikail spoke passionately about the power of collective bargaining, of how a unified voice could force the management to improve working conditions and offer fairer wages. He described similar movements in other cities, successful strikes that had garnered concessions from greedy factory owners.

Jurgis listened intently, a sense of possibility swirling within him. This wasn't just about survival anymore; it was about fighting for a better life, for a future where their labor was valued and respected. He shared his experience of standing up for the young worker, the silent approval from his fellow Lithuanians.

A fire seemed to ignite within the group. Jurgis' story resonated with them, a testament to the strength that lay dormant within the downtrodden workers. They discussed strategies, discreet ways to spread the word about the union amongst the diverse immigrant population.

The risk was high. Management had a ruthless reputation for crushing any dissent, firing instigators without a second thought. Yet, the potential rewards were even higher. A chance to rewrite the brutal narrative of Packingtown, to carve out a space where dignity and fair treatment were not just words but a lived reality.

Jurgis left the meeting feeling a newfound sense of purpose. He was no longer just a nameless shoveler; he was a part of something bigger, a growing wave of resistance. He knew the road ahead would be fraught with danger, but the seed of hope had been planted.

The next morning, Jurgis approached Lefty, the one-eyed veteran, with a hesitant question.

"Have you heard anything... about a union?"

Lefty's face hardened, his gaze sweeping the surrounding area. He leaned in close, his voice a raspy whisper. "There's always whispers," he said. "Be careful where you speak them."

Jurgis nodded, the weight of the secret settling on him. He knew the risks, but he also knew the potential rewards. He would spread the word with caution, finding fertile ground amongst his fellow Lithuanians, planting the seeds of rebellion one conversation at a time.

The heart of Packingtown might be a place of darkness and despair, but a spark of hope had ignited. It was a flicker, fragile and uncertain, but one that Jurgis and his newfound comrades would nurture, fanning it into a flame that could illuminate the path towards a brighter future. The battle for justice had begun, and Jurgis, the once reluctant shoveler, was now a reluctant, but determined, soldier in the fight.

Chapter 4: A Glimpse of Hope

Weeks bled into months, the harsh monotony of Packingtown settling into a rhythm that Jurgis found himself begrudgingly accepting. His body, hardened by relentless labor, ached less, though the stench of death clung to him like a shroud. He had become a cog in the brutal machine, his dreams of a thriving carpentry business relegated to a dusty corner of his mind.

Yet, a spark of defiance flickered within him. The whispers of a union, a movement of resistance against the oppressive working conditions, had taken root. Jurgis, along with Mikail and a growing network of discontented workers, became the clandestine gardeners of this rebellion, carefully nurturing the seeds of dissent.

Their meetings were shrouded in secrecy, held under the dim glow of flickering gas lamps in back alleys and cramped tenement rooms. The air crackled with a mix of fear and hope as they discussed strategies, translating Mikail's impassioned Polish speeches into Lithuanian, Yiddish, and other languages spoken by the diverse immigrant population.

News of the union traveled like wildfire through the boarding houses and saloons frequented by the workers. Whispers turned to murmured discussions, and soon, a sense of solidarity began to solidify. The faces of the men around Jurgis, once etched with fatigue and resignation, now held a glimmer of defiance.

One crisp autumn morning, a sense of unease hung heavy in the air. Rumors swirled that the management had caught wind of the union activity. A sense of paranoia gripped the workers as they filed into the slaughterhouse, the usual banter replaced by a tense silence.

Jurgis, his stomach churning with a blend of fear and anticipation, scanned the faces around him. Would this be the day management cracked down? Would their months of clandestine organizing be crushed under the iron fist of the packers?

As the workday progressed, the tension remained. Foremen seemed to scrutinize the workers with an extra layer of suspicion. Every hushed conversation or stolen glance drew a scowl or a barked order. Jurgis felt like he was walking a tightrope, the threat of exposure hanging heavy over his head.

Around noon, a commotion erupted from one of the processing areas. A young Italian immigrant, barely a teenager, had been caught talking with a fellow worker. The foreman, a man known for his brutality, grabbed the young man by the scruff of his neck and dragged him towards the exit.

A collective gasp rippled through the workers. Jurgis watched in horror as the foreman shoved the young man out into the open, yelling something about "troublemakers" and "being sent packing."

Suddenly, a voice boomed from the back of the room. It was Mikail, his voice filled with a righteous anger. "This is not right! We will not stand for this anymore!"

Silence descended. All eyes turned towards Mikail, a lone figure standing tall against the backdrop of fear. The tension in the room was thick enough to cut with a knife. Jurgis felt a bead of sweat roll down his forehead. Was this it? Was Mikail about to spark the fire they had been so carefully stoking?

Jurgis' heart hammered in his chest, a frantic drumbeat echoing the pounding in his ears. Mikail's words hung in the air, a defiant challenge to the oppressive silence that had ruled

Packingtown for so long. Every eye remained fixed on the Polish organizer, waiting for his next move.

The foreman, a man built like a bull with a face perpetually contorted in a sneer, turned towards Mikail, a vein pulsing in his forehead. "What did you say, Polak?" he snarled, his voice laced with menace.

Mikail stood his ground, his gaze unwavering. "We will not tolerate this mistreatment any longer!" he declared, his voice ringing through the vast hall. "We deserve fair wages, safer working conditions, and respect!"

A murmur rippled through the crowd. Some workers, emboldened by Mikail's courage, nodded in agreement. Others, still fearful of retribution, remained silent, their expressions betraying a flicker of hope mixed with apprehension.

Jurgis, his hands clenched into fists at his side, felt a surge of adrenaline course through him. This was it. The moment they had been preparing for, the moment of truth.

Before the foreman could react, another voice joined Mikail's chorus. It was Lefty, the one-eyed veteran, his voice hoarse but firm. "He speaks the truth," Lefty rasped. "We've had enough of this abuse!"

One by one, more voices joined in. A chorus of discontent, a cacophony of languages, all united in a single purpose. The room thrummed with a raw energy that Jurgis had never witnessed before.

The foreman's face contorted in rage. He sputtered, spewing threats and insults, but his voice was drowned out by the growing tide of defiance. The workers, for the first time, felt a sense of collective power, a feeling of solidarity that transcended their individual fears.

Suddenly, a whistle shrilled through the air, its piercing sound temporarily silencing the crowd. All eyes turned towards the source of the sound – the office doorway, where Mr. Grimes, the notoriously ruthless plant manager, stood with a grim expression etched on his face.

Grimes, a man with a thick neck and a perpetual scowl, was known for his iron fist and intolerance for dissent. His presence sent a wave of apprehension through the room, the fragile unity threatening to crumble under his harsh gaze.

Jurgis held his breath, waiting for the inevitable storm. Would Grimes crack down with brutal force, snuffing out their nascent rebellion before it could truly take root?

Silence descended upon the slaughterhouse once more, thick and suffocating. The workers, their voices hoarse from their outburst, watched with bated breath as Mr. Grimes surveyed the scene. His gaze swept across the room, taking in the defiant faces and the simmering anger. Jurgis felt a bead of sweat trickle down his temple, the air thick with anticipation.

Grimes, puffing on a cigar that seemed permanently attached to his lips, exhaled a plume of smoke. His voice, when it finally came, was a low growl that resonated throughout the room. "So," he drawled, his eyes narrowed, "this is the trouble I've been hearing about."

Mikail, unfazed by the manager's imposing presence, stepped forward. "This isn't trouble, Mr. Grimes," he countered, his voice surprisingly steady. "This is a group of men simply asking for fair treatment."

A murmur of approval rippled through the crowd. Jurgis felt a surge of pride in Mikail's boldness. Here was a leader, a man who dared to stand up to the tyrant that was Mr. Grimes.

Grimes stared at Mikail for a long moment, his eyes seeming to bore holes into the Polish organizer. Then, a flicker of something akin to surprise crossed his face. Perhaps, Jurgis thought with a jolt, they had caught the manager off guard with their sudden display of unity. Perhaps, just perhaps, they had a chance.

"Fair treatment, huh?" Grimes scoffed, his voice laced with disdain. "This ain't a charity, folks. This is a business. And business needs to run smoothly."

He pointed his cigar at the crowd, his voice dripping with sarcasm. "You think you can just stop working whenever you like? You think the world will stop turning if you don't like the smell of blood and guts?"

A voice boomed from the back. It was Dede Antanas, his weathered face creased with determination. "We ain't asking for handouts, Mr. Grimes," he said, his voice surprisingly strong. "We're asking for what we deserve. A living wage, decent working conditions, and a little respect for our bodies and our families."

The crowd erupted in a chorus of agreement. Jurgis felt a surge of energy course through him. They weren't backing down. They had tasted the power of their collective voice, and they wouldn't surrender it easily.

Grimes watched the scene unfold, his face unreadable. He seemed to be weighing his options, calculating his next move. This wasn't the usual docile workforce he was accustomed to dealing with. Would he choose to crush them outright, or could there be a way to maintain control without resorting to brute force?

The tension in the room was palpable. Time seemed to stretch and distort as everyone waited for Grimes' decision.

Would this be the end of their fledgling movement, or could they somehow find a way to negotiate, to carve out a semblance of dignity within the brutal confines of Packingtown? The answer, hanging in the balance, would determine the fate of their rebellion and the future of their lives.

The standoff continued, the air thick with anticipation. Grimes, his face a mask of conflicting emotions, surveyed the defiant crowd. The workers, emboldened by their newfound solidarity, remained resolute. Jurgis felt a knot of anxiety tightening in his stomach. Would their courage hold, or would they crumble under the pressure?

Finally, Grimes broke the silence. He stubbed out his cigar with a forceful twist, the hiss echoing in the cavernous space. "Alright, listen up," he barked, his voice surprisingly mild. "I ain't deaf. I hear your complaints. But this ain't the time or place for a negotiation."

A wave of disappointment washed over Jurgis. Was this it? Was their rebellion being snuffed out before it could truly take root?

Grimes continued, his voice laced with a hint of grudging respect. "However," he said, "I'm a reasonable man. You folks seem to have some...concerns. So, I'm willing to listen."

He gestured towards Mikail. "You, the spokesman. Come to my office tomorrow afternoon. We'll have a little chat. See if we can find some...accommodations."

The crowd exchanged surprised glances. Was this a trick? A ploy to single out Mikail and quash the movement? Or was there a genuine possibility for compromise?

Jurgis saw a flicker of suspicion in Mikail's eyes. He knew the risks of entering the lion's den alone. Yet, he also saw a glimmer of hope. A chance, however slim, to improve their working conditions through negotiation rather than outright defiance.

"Alright, Mr. Grimes," Mikail said, his voice steady. "I'll be there."

A murmur of approval rippled through the crowd. This wasn't a victory, not yet. But it wasn't a defeat either. They had held their ground, they had forced Mr. Grimes to acknowledge their grievances. And most importantly, they had taken a step, a small but significant step, towards a future where their voices could be heard, their needs considered.

Grimes, with a curt nod, turned and retreated back into his office. The tension slowly began to dissipate, replaced by a cautious optimism. The workers, their initial anger tempered by a sense of accomplishment, filed out of the slaughterhouse, their heads held a little higher than usual.

Jurgis walked alongside Mikail and Lefty, a wave of relief washing over him. They had faced down Mr. Grimes, and they were still standing. Tomorrow, the real challenge would begin. The negotiation. But for now, they had a reason to celebrate – a flicker of hope had ignited in the heart of Packingtown, a spark that refused to be extinguished.

"We did it," Jurgis whispered, a nervous smile playing on his lips.

Mikail nodded, a grim look on his face. "We did," he said. "But this is just the beginning. The real fight starts tomorrow."

Jurgis knew he was right. The path ahead wouldn't be easy. It would be fraught with danger, with setbacks and possible betrayals. But for the first time since arriving in Packingtown, Jurgis felt a sliver of hope. They weren't just individuals anymore, they were a collective force, a union of discontent with the potential to rewrite the narrative of their lives. And that, in the brutal heart of Packingtown, was a reason to fight for a brighter future.

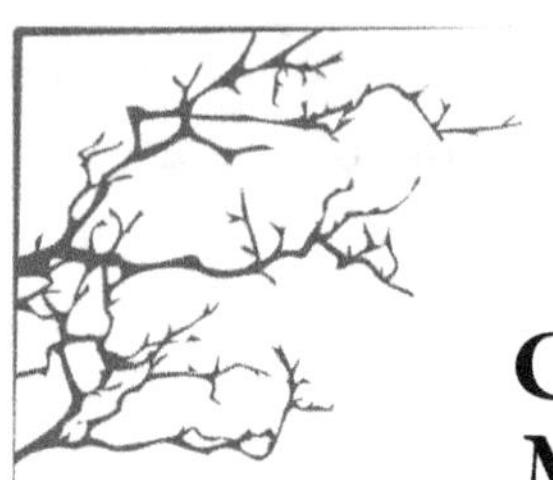

Chapter 5: A Mountain of Furniture

The news of Mikail's meeting with Mr. Grimes spread like wildfire through the boarding houses and saloons of Packingtown. The workers, their initial fear replaced by a cautious optimism, awaited with bated breath for any scrap of information.

Jurgis, unable to shake off the nervous excitement, found himself pacing the cramped confines of their tenement apartment. Ona, her face etched with worry, watched him with concern. Dede Antanas, ever the stoic observer, puffed on his pipe, his silence more eloquent than any words.

The next day crawled by like an eternity. Every creak of the floorboards, every knock on the door, sent Jurgis' heart pounding in his chest. Finally, as the sun dipped below the horizon, casting long shadows across the grimy streets, the door creaked open.

Mikail entered, a weary smile etched on his face. Relief washed over Jurgis, a wave so powerful it nearly knocked him off his feet. Mikail wasn't alone, which was a good sign. He was accompanied by Lefty, whose one good eye held a glimmer of cautious satisfaction.

"Well?" Jurgis blurted out, unable to contain his impatience.

Mikail took a deep breath, his voice raspy from a long day of negotiation. "We got something," he announced. The room held its collective breath. "Not everything we wanted, mind you, but it's a start."

He explained in detail the terms Mr. Grimes had offered. A slight increase in wages, a reduction in the most grueling aspects of the shoveling work, and the promise of investigating safer working conditions.

It wasn't a complete victory, not by a long shot. The wages remained meager, the work would still be dangerous, and there was no guarantee of Mr. Grimes following through on his promises. But for the workers of Packingtown, it was a significant concession, a crack in the ironclad control they had endured for so long.

A wave of discussion erupted in the cramped apartment. Some, like Jurgis, were cautiously optimistic, seeing the potential for further improvements. Others, like Dede Antanas, remained skeptical, wary of Mr. Grimes' motives. The debate went on for hours, fueled by a mixture of hope and apprehension.

Finally, exhaustion settled over the group. As they settled into their makeshift beds, the weight of the day pressed down on them. Jurgis, despite the doubts lingering at the edge of his mind, felt a spark of hope flicker within him. They had achieved something, however small. They had shown their strength, their willingness to fight for a better life.

The next morning, news of the tentative agreement spread through Packingtown like wildfire. The mood amongst the workers, though still cautious, was noticeably lighter. They held their heads a little higher, their steps a little more purposeful. The tentative victory, a testament to their newfound solidarity, had instilled a sense of empowerment in them.

However, Jurgis knew that this was just the beginning. The fight for fair treatment, for safe working conditions, and for a living wage was far from over. But for now, they had a reason to celebrate – a small but significant victory in the heart of Packingtown.

The euphoria of their minor victory faded quickly under the harsh realities of Packingtown. The increased wages, though a welcome change, barely covered the rising costs of rent and food. The promised changes in work duties seemed slow to materialize, leaving the men skeptical of Mr. Grimes' commitment.

Yet, a subtle shift had taken place. The whispers of unionism had become more vocal, a constant murmur beneath the surface of daily life. Jurgis, emboldened by their recent success, found himself spreading the word amongst his Lithuanian compatriots, urging them to stay united, to remain vigilant.

One evening, as they huddled around a meager meal of boiled potatoes and watery stew, Ona brought up a topic that had been nagging at her. "We need furniture, Jurgis," she said, her voice laced with frustration. "This bare floor and these rickety crates are no way to live."

Jurgis winced. He knew she was right. Their cramped apartment, devoid of any comfort, was a constant reminder of their poverty. He longed to provide for his family, to create a haven within the chaos of Packingtown.

"I know," he sighed, guilt gnawing at him. "But with the meager wages..."

Dede Antanas, ever the pragmatist, puffed on his pipe and offered a suggestion. "There are advertisements plastered everywhere," he rasped, his voice gravelly. "They offer furniture on credit, affordable payments they say."

Jurgis had seen those advertisements. They were plastered on every wall, promising easy solutions to their problems. But the stories of debt and repossession that circulated amongst the workers filled him with a sense of unease.

"It's a trap," Lefty chimed in, his gruff voice filled with caution. "They lure you in with low payments, then bury you in debt. You end up working twice as hard for those bloodsuckers."

Ona's face fell, her dream of a furnished home seemingly dashed. Jurgis, however, felt a spark of determination ignite within him. He wouldn't let debt be their only option.

The next day, after a grueling shift at the slaughterhouse, Jurgis set out on a mission. He combed through the labyrinthine streets of Packingtown, his eyes scanning the endless advertisements. Finally, tucked away in a small, dusty corner, he found it – a notice for a used furniture sale.

Hope surged through him. Perhaps, just perhaps, there was a way to furnish their home without succumbing to the clutches of loan sharks. He hurried back to the tenement, his heart pounding with anticipation.

The sale was a chaotic affair, held in a dimly lit warehouse overflowing with discarded furniture. Jurgis, his bargaining skills honed by his days navigating the harsh realities of Packingtown, managed to secure a rickety table, a few mismatched chairs, and a creaky bed frame – all at a price he could barely afford.

The journey back to the tenement was arduous, but Jurgis barely felt the weight of the furniture. He carried with him the promise of a furnished home, a small step towards a semblance of normalcy within the chaos of their lives.

That evening, with Ona and Dede Antanas lending a hand, they assembled their meager furniture. The rickety table wobbled, the chairs creaked precariously, and the bed frame looked like it could collapse at any moment. Yet, as they surveyed their handiwork, a sense of warmth filled the cramped apartment.

It wasn't perfect, far from it. But it was theirs. A symbol of their resilience, their determination to build a life, however humble, within the unforgiving heart of Packingtown. As Ona lit a few candles, casting a warm glow on their meager furnishings, Jurgis felt a flicker of pride. They were still poor, still struggling, but they were together, and they had hope. The fight for a better life continued, but for tonight, they would celebrate their small victory, their furnished dream, in the heart of darkness.

Life in Packingtown continued to be a relentless grind. The days stretched into weeks, then months, a monotonous cycle of backbreaking labor, foul smells, and aching muscles. Yet, a subtle shift had taken root within the community. The whispers of unionism had morphed into a quiet hum, a shared understanding simmering beneath the surface.

Jurgis, his initial optimism tempered by the harsh realities of Packingtown, remained a vocal advocate for the movement. He found himself drawn not only to the menfolk struggling for better working conditions, but also to the plight of the women.

The women of Packingtown, often overlooked or underestimated, toiled long hours in sweatshops and canneries, enduring conditions as harsh as those in the slaughterhouses. They were the seamstresses stitching clothes for a pittance, the cannery workers hunched over conveyor belts, their hands raw from handling acidic fruit.

One evening, as Jurgis and Ona sat huddled by a flickering candle, Ona confided in him. "There's a woman at the sweatshop," she whispered, her voice laced with concern. "A young girl, barely more than a child. They work her to the bone, pay her a pittance, and treat her with no respect."

Jurgis' heart clenched. He knew Ona spoke the truth. The stories of exploitation within the sweatshops were rife. Young girls, lured by the promise of work, were often forced into grueling labor for meager wages.

A seed of an idea began to sprout in Jurgis' mind. The union, initially focused on the men in the slaughterhouses, could be a force for good for everyone. The women, with their shared struggles and vulnerabilities, could be a powerful addition to their movement.

The next day, Jurgis approached Mikail, his voice filled with a newfound determination. "We need to talk," he said. "It's not just the men suffering here. The women..."

He explained the hardships faced by the women of Packingtown, the exploitation in the sweatshops, the long hours for meager pay. Mikail listened intently, a thoughtful frown creasing his brow.

"You're right, Jurgis," he said finally. "Our fight for better working conditions needs to encompass everyone. The women are just as vital a part of this workforce as the men. They deserve fair treatment and a voice just as much as we do."

Thus began a quiet campaign of outreach. Jurgis, with Ona translating and providing support, began approaching the women at the sweatshops and canneries. They spoke in hushed tones, sharing stories of hardship and exploitation, planting the seeds of solidarity.

The women, initially hesitant, were gradually drawn in by the promise of a collective voice. They saw their own struggles reflected in the stories of the men. Together, they could be a force to be reckoned with.

Slowly, a network of women began to emerge. They met in secret, sharing stories of abuse and dreaming of a better future.

The whispers of unionism morphed into a chorus, a unified voice demanding change.

The inclusion of the women brought a new dimension to the movement. Their stories of hardship were heartbreaking, their resilience inspiring. They brought a different perspective, a different kind of strength to the fight for justice in Packingtown.

Jurgis, witnessing the quiet courage of the women, felt a renewed sense of purpose. The fight for a better life wasn't just for the men in the slaughterhouses. It was for all of them – the men, the women, the children – a fight for a future where their voices could be heard, their dignity respected, and their labor valued. The heart of Packingtown, once a place of darkness and despair, now harbored a flicker of hope, a growing fire fueled by the collective yearning for a better tomorrow.

The movement, now a unified force encompassing both men and women, felt like a living organism, growing stronger with each whispered conversation and clandestine meeting. Jurgis, along with Mikail and Ona, became the nucleus of this organism, spreading the message of solidarity and urging workers to join their cause.

One crisp autumn evening, a flyer announcing a secret meeting for all Packingtown workers found its way into the hands of nearly everyone. The message was simple – a unified front could force meaningful concessions from Mr. Grimes and the management. The response was overwhelming.

The designated meeting place was a dimly lit tavern located on the outskirts of Packingtown, a haven for immigrants and a far cry from the opulent saloons frequented by the city's elite. The air crackled with nervous energy as men and women, from diverse backgrounds and various industries, filled the room.

Jurgis, his heart pounding in his chest, scanned the faces around him. He saw fear, yes, but also a steely determination. These were people who had endured unimaginable hardships, and they were no longer willing to be silent.

Mikail, standing on a makeshift platform, took charge. He spoke of the injustice they all faced, the grueling labor for meager wages, the unsafe working conditions, and the blatant disregard for their basic humanity.

He then spoke of their power, their collective voice. He explained the concept of a strike, a unified walkout that would cripple Packingtown's industries and force Mr. Grimes to negotiate. A low murmur rippled through the crowd. The idea, once unthinkable, now seemed like a possibility, however risky.

One by one, others took the floor. A young Italian woman recounted the horrendous conditions at the cannery, her voice trembling but resolute. A grizzled Irish dockworker spoke of the dangers of his job and the lack of safety measures. Each story was a testament to the suffering they endured, a stark reminder of why they needed to act.

By the end of the night, the room vibrated with a newfound determination. They voted to move forward with the strike, a one-day walkout to send a clear message to Mr. Grimes. The date was set – two weeks hence, enough time to spread the word and ensure maximum participation.

Jurgis, leaving the tavern with Ona by his side, felt a mix of exhilaration and fear. They were taking a bold step, one that could potentially change their lives forever. The road ahead wouldn't be easy. There would be threats, intimidation, and perhaps even violence from Mr. Grimes and his goons. But looking at the steely glint in Ona's eyes, Jurgis knew they weren't alone.

The heart of Packingtown, once a place of drudgery and despair, now thundered with a unified heartbeat. The whispers of rebellion had become a roar, a collective voice demanding justice. The fight for a better future had begun, and the workers, united in their desire for change, were ready to face whatever came their way. The strike loomed large on the horizon, and Packingtown was about to witness the unwavering power of solidarity.

About the Author

Mrigendra Bharti, born on June 29, 2004, in South Delhi, India, is a multifaceted individual recognized as the owner of Mrigendra Bharti Group InfoTech India Co. Pvt Ltd. Beyond his entrepreneurial endeavors, he is a distinguished music producer, director, and a budding writer.

Embarking on his professional journey at a young age, Mrigendra Bharti's visionary leadership has led to the establishment of several successful ventures, including Croma Music Series Entertainment, Sellbrochure, Fauget Innovative, and more.

What sets Mrigendra apart is his early initiation into the world of business. His foray into the unknown realms of entrepreneurship began during his 10th-grade years, where he delved into the music industry. This initial venture laid the foundation for subsequent achievements, showcasing his dedication and resilience.

Having honed his skills in music, Mrigendra Bharti not only demonstrated significant growth in his craft but also expanded his professional network. His passion extends beyond music, encompassing app and website development, as well as graphic design.

Fueled by his creative aspirations, Mrigendra established the Mrigendra Bharti Group, a company specializing in website and app development. Currently, he collaborates with a dedicated team, collectively working on ambitious projects that promise innovation and excellence.

Mrigendra's journey serves as an inspiration, particularly for today's students, highlighting the potential of youthful determination and the ability to transform innovative ideas into successful businesses. As he continues to make strides in various domains, Mrigendra Bharti remains a dynamic force, contributing vibrancy to the realms of business, music, and technology.

Read more at https://www.imwriter-mrigendra.rf.gd.